The Adventures of Goldilocks and Baby Bear

What Happened Next

by Linda Hepner

DORRANCE
PUBLISHING CO
EST. 1920
PITTSBURGH, PENNSYLVANIA 15238

Dorrance Publishing Co
585 Alpha Drive
Suite 103
Pittsburgh, PA 15238
Visit our website at *www.dorrancebookstore.com*

ISBN: 978-1-6366-1337-6
eISBN: 978-1-6366-1916-3

For Amitai until he was 5,
for Melvyn in 1945, and for Gershy for 55 years

The Adventures of Goldilocks and Baby Bear

What Happened Next

Goldilocks and the Eight Hundred and Eighty-Eight Socks

When Goldilocks ran home crying, she found her mother washing eight hundred and eighty-eight socks in the big garden tub.

Her mother was the champion socks washer, and never lost a single one. Every summer, everyone in the town brought her their socks to wash. First she stirred the huge pot with a long paddle, and then she poured out the water onto an old sheet on the grass. When all the socks had fallen into a heap, she put them out to dry. Soon there were socks hanging from the apple tree, the cherry tree and the lilac bushes, on the wheelbarrow, the swing, and on the garden gate.

Goldilocks asked, "Can I help you?"

Her mother replied, "Oh no, thank you, but where have you been?"

"Oh, nowhere," replied Goldilocks. Then she began crying again.

"Hmm," said her mother, "I think you need to tell me what happened!"

"Oh Mom," Goldilocks sobbed, "I went to say hello to that new Bear family, but they scared me!"

"What did they do?" asked her mother.

"They woke me up and shouted!" said Goldilocks.

"Why were you asleep?"

"Well…." Goldilocks replied and told her the story, which of course you already know. If you don't, here, briefly, is what happened.

Goldilocks, who was a very inquisitive little girl, went down the road to the cottage where the Bear Family had just moved in. She knocked on the door, and when there was no answer, she opened it and walked into the tidy kitchen. Strike One! On the table she saw three bowls of porridge. She poked her finger into the biggest bowl. Strike Two! But owee! *The porridge burned her finger, it was so hot. The middle-sized bowl was too cold, so she pushed it away and spilled it over the table. Strike Three! The little bowl with the pictures of lambs on it was just right, so she found a spoon and ate it all up. That was Strike Four, and after it came Strikes Five, Six, and Seven: Goldilocks tried out three chairs. The highest was too big, the middle-sized was too low, and the smallest was exactly right; but being a lively girl and not a quiet little bear, when Goldilocks sat down, it broke, so that she fell on the floor. Then she climbed upstairs and found three neatly made beds (Strikes Eight, Nine, and Ten). The biggest was too hard, the middle-sized too soft, and the littlest just right, so (Strike Eleven!) she lay down and fell asleep.*

The Three Bears came home from exploring the woods across the road. Papa Bear growled, "Who's been eating my porridge?" and Mama Bear exclaimed, "Who…! (etc.)" and Baby Bear squealed, "…and somebody has eaten all of it!" The three chairs were all examined and Baby Bear cried when he saw that his had been broken into pieces. They all trooped upstairs to find the burglar, and there lay a pretty golden-haired girl, fast asleep in Baby Bear's bed.

"Someone's in my bed!" yelled Baby Bear. His parents rushed in to see. Goldilocks woke up, and was so terrified that she rushed downstairs, out of the house and all the way home, crying.

Goldilocks's mother said, "They must be really upset too! You have to go back and say you're sorry."

Goldilocks stamped her feet. "*They* have to say that *they* are sorry! They scared me!"

"No," replied her mom. "You went into their house. Did they invite you? No. Did they say, *Come any time and eat our porridge?* No. *Break our furniture? Mess up our beds?*"

"Oh dear," Goldilocks wept. "I can't go! They might eat me!"

"Nonsense," said her mom. "Help me sort these last hundred socks and we will go together."

Soon Daddy Goldie came home. He heard what had happened and found a big bottle of blackberry cordial he had made from berries in the woods.

"We will all go," he said, "and meet our new neighbors."

They set out, Daddy and Mommy Goldie, and Goldilocks, who was five.

When they reached the Bears' cottage, they knocked and Papa Bear opened it.

"Hello!" he said. "Can I help you?"

Daddy Goldie said, "We are the Goldie Family, your new neighbors down the road, and want to say 'Welcome' to you!"

He handed them the bottle of blackberry cordial and Papa Bear said, "What a nice surprise! Do come in!"

Then he noticed Goldilocks hiding behind her mom.

"Oh ho," he roared. "We have already met!"

"I am very, very sorry!" Goldilocks cried, trying to slip away.

"Ha ha ha!" laughed Papa Bear. "We are sorry we scared YOU! We called for you to come back, but you ran away too fast!"

At that moment Mama Bear came to the door and cried out, "Oh, the pretty little girl who runs as fast as a hare! Please come in!"

Baby Bear came jumping down the stairs, and Mama said, "Now, Baby, here is a new friend. Go pick some mulberries and show her your toys!"

Baby Bear walked into the yard and Goldilocks followed. "I am sorry I broke your chair," she said.

"I'm sorry I scared you!" said Baby Bear. "Do girls like climbing trees?"

"I love climbing trees," Goldilocks answered, and the two new friends pulled themselves up a mulberry tree. They sat on a low branch and picked mulberries until Baby's fur and Goldilocks's face were all smeared with purple. They laughed until Goldilocks fell off into a puddle. She stood up and called out, "I'm fine!" Baby Bear slid down and they played hide'n'seek.

When they went indoors, Mommy Goldie sighed, "Oh dear, your pink shirt and socks are all purple. Please remember that you are not a bear, you are a girl! What will our new friends think of you?"

Mama Bear interrupted, "We think she is a nice girl and she can come to play whenever she wants, but please, Goldilocks, knock on the door first!"

The next morning Goldilocks woke early, and as no one else was awake, she opened the window and climbed down into the garden. She picked some raspberries in her mother's berry patch and ran down the road alongside the wood that led to the Bears' house. She knocked very softly. No one was awake there either, so she threw some twigs at Baby Bear's window and soon he looked out.

"I have raspberries!" she called. Baby Bear came downstairs and they sat eating and playing knuckle-bone games on the doorstep. After a while Papa Bear came out.

"Little girl," he roared, "I see you aren't afraid of us anymore. Does your mommy know you are here?"

"No," replied Goldilocks, "but she never cares what I do because everything turns out fine!"

At that moment Daddy Goldie came racing down along the road.

"I thought she'd be here," he exclaimed. "She is always up to mischief, this girl!"

"Let them play in the garden," suggested Papa Bear, "and you come in for some breakfast. Mama has made some blackberry flavored porridge!"

Daddy went inside, and Goldilocks said, "Let's explore the forest!"

Baby Bear said, "A forest! I thought it was just a wood!"

"This is the bushy wood," Goldilocks replied, "but deep inside, it becomes a forest! I have always wanted to see it!"

"I'm too scared," whispered Baby Bear. "I'm only five."

"I'm five too," said Goldilocks, "and five and five make ten, so we will be fine!"

The two friends slipped out of the garden, walked across the road and deep into the wood to where the forest began.

The trees rustled and the twigs under their feet crackled. Silly little squirrels poked their noses out of tree trunks and called to each other, "Watch out! Bear coming!" but Wise Owl opened one eye and hooted, "Don't worry about the little bear! Worry about that little girl!"

The silly squirrels knew they had better hide from Wise Owl, so they scuttled between the leaves.

Some white rabbits hopped out of their holes and Goldilocks chased them calling, "Come back, little rabbits, I want to hold you!" Baby Bear saw two huge eyes looking at him over a bush and quickly scrambled up an oak tree.

"Come down!" shouted Goldilocks. "That was just Dear Deer!"

Baby Bear pretended to be brave and said, "I didn't want to scare her, because my dad always says, 'Don't frighten wild animals!'"

Wise Owl flew over and sat near Baby Bear. "Your dad is right. But you are an animal too, and you don't seem very wild to me. Where do you Bears come from?"

"We come from a zoo," replied Baby Bear politely. "We were treated very well by Humans and were sent out to live in the world and teach People that we are people too."

Wise Owl said, "They have learned a good lesson, and to you I say, good luck."

He closed one eye, opened the other and added, "Have fun, but choose good friends." Then he turned his head round in his feathers and pretended to sleep.

Meantime, Goldilocks was petting Dear Deer and climbing on her back, saying, "Help me step up into the tree!"

Deer complained, "Goldilocks, you are not three years old anymore, you are getting heavy!"

Goldilocks grabbed a low bough and swung into the tree right next to Baby Bear. Climbing up was easy. They pulled themselves to the highest leafy branch way above the ground and clambered along it on all fours. The branch thought to itself, "My, that's a heavy load today!" and swayed downwards. The two friends held on tight and Goldilocks laughed, "Let's swing!"

Baby Bear said, "Oh no, don't you know the song, 'Rockabye Baby'?"

Goldilocks sang the song, and at "...when the bough breaks," she bounced, and the branch swung up and down, groaning.

"Stop, Goldilocks!" cried Baby Bear. "We will fall down!"

"We'll be fine!" shouted Goldilocks. "This is such fun!"

"Bother," thought the branch. "I'm going to break... I must get them off!" It swayed faster and Baby Bear clambered back along the branch, down the trunk of the tree and onto a wild strawberry patch.

Goldilocks called, "How did you do that?"

Bear answered, "I have claws! And I'm a bear! I can get up and down!"

Goldilocks crawled even farther along the branch. Then she held on tight with both hands and looked down. How high she was! Where was Dear Deer to climb onto like a step? "I will fall!" she called.

The squirrels and rabbits came to watch. "Jump!" rattled the squirrels. "Hop!" squealed the rabbits. "Fly!" chirped some birds on another tree.

Baby Bear found some wild strawberries and began eating them. "Save some for me," called Goldilocks. Baby Bear threw a few to her but she couldn't let go of the branch and her arms began to ache. "Drop down!" squealed the squirrels. "It won't hurt!" She was just about to let herself go, when voices came through the trees and she heard her father calling her; "Goldilocks! Where are you?" and Papa Bear calling "Baby! Baby!"

Baby Bear shouted, "We're here!"

"Where is 'here'?"

"By the big tree!"

"Which big tree?"

"Wise Owl's tree!"

Wise Owl, who did not like crowds, lifted himself with a mere whoosh of his wings and flew away, calling to all the other birds, "Come on, Flying Company, come with me."

Daddy and Papa Bear came pushing through the trees and saw Baby Bear eating strawberries, several little rabbits and squirrels on the grass, a worried hedgehog, and some grouse who couldn't fly. "Mr. Goldie, help Miss Goldilocks!" they all chorused, but Daddy Goldie, looking up, could only see her feet in socks far above, dangling through the leaves.

"Do you have a very long ladder?" he asked Papa Bear.

"No!" came the answer.

"Then we will have to get Fireman Jim! Hold on, girl, it might be quite a while before he gets here!"

Goldilocks cried out, "Daddy, I'm going to swing like a monkey and then drop down, catch me!"

"Don't!" squawked the grouse.

"Do!" squealed the rabbits.

"Whizz away!" buzzed some passing dragonflies.

Papa Bear said, "I will stand underneath so that she can fall on top of my fur."

Daddy Goldie said, "Thank you, but there are too many branches in the way. She will crash down in the wrong place."

A voice came out of the wood and Noble Stag walked towards them. "My daughter Dear Deer is bringing help," he said.

Unknown to them, Dear Deer had run to town as fast as she could and told Fireman Jim to bring his long ladder as quickly as possible. He tried, but could not drive his fire engine into the wood.

"I will have to come back!" he shouted, and drove away, clanging his bell.

Before long, everyone heard a loud hacking, clonking helicopter noise above the trees. The alarmed animals rushed out of sight. Fireman Jim leaned out of his cockpit and shouted, "I cannot land, there's no room! I will drop down a rope! Goldilocks, catch it!"

He threw down the rope but it got stuck in the branches at the top of the trees.

"I will have to find someone to help me come back later with the ladder!" he shouted down, and chugged away.

Goldilocks called, "I'm slipping!"

Papa Bear said, "I'm coming up to rescue you!"

He began climbing but the branch Goldilocks was on was too high and thin to hold him.

Baby Bear said, "I will try," and climbed up again. He could not climb along the branch to Goldilocks, so he said, "We will just have to wait until Fireman Jim comes here with his ladder!"

The branch Goldilocks was on groaned to them, "I will bend and sway, but I will try hard not to break!"

They waited and waited. Mama Bear and Mommy Goldie arrived looking up anxiously. Baby Bear and Goldilocks made up jokes.

"Knock knock!" *"Who's there?"* "Berry!" *"Berry Who?"* "Berry berry hungry!"

"Knock knock!" *"Who's there?"* "Bunny!" *"Bunny Who?"* "Bunny joke!"

"Knock knock..." and at that a strange fluttering noise came nearer over their heads. When they looked up, their eyes grew wide with astonishment.

The sky was full of flying colors, brought lower and lower by hundreds of little birds, each carrying what looked like long thin flags waving behind them as they dived through the trees and landed on the ground beneath the groaning branch. With them came Wise Owl himself, calling orders, "This way! Drop the yellow ones here! The blue ones there! Now make a pile!"

The animals and the people on the ground looked on in amazement as the birds dropped their flags and the entire ground became thick with...

Mommy Goldie cried, "The socks! The socks! The birds have brought all our socks!"

Everyone began cheering. Goldilocks peered down and the ground was as colorful as a patchwork quilt. She slid over the branch a little until she saw only some thin twigs in the way and then let go, falling and crashing through the leaves onto the soft hill of socks on the ground.

Her mom and dad rushed over calling, "Are you all right?"

Goldilocks picked herself up, saying, "I'm fine!"

Baby Bear bounded over and hugged her. All the grownups frowned.

"We are glad you are fine," they all said, "But always remember, what goes up must come down!"

"Thank you everyone," said Goldilocks, "but you see, everything turned out fine in the end. It always does!"

"Oh, this story isn't finished yet," said Mommy Goldie. "We have to bring all these socks back to the neighbors!"

Goldilocks said, "The birds can do that!"

The birds nodded. Wise Owl said to them, "Flying Company! Take back the socks!" The birds fluttered down, picked up the socks, and flew away.

The two families thanked everyone and walked back to the Bears' house. On the way they met Fireman Jim and his son Jim Junior carrying the long ladder.

"Come with us for lunch!" cried Papa Bear.

All the People, Stag, and Dear Deer, followed by some of the squirrels and several rabbits, crowded into the Bears' garden, and Mama Bear brought everyone cookies and blackberries. When lunch was over, the Goldie family walked back down the road to their home.

"Oh no!" said Mommy Goldie. "You have a job to do!" There in the front yard the birds had dumped an enormous pile of socks, but once again they were all mixed up. "Sort out all these socks, Goldilocks, and no playing until they are all in pairs!"

"Oh no!" cried Goldilocks.

"Oh yes!" answered her mother. Then, laughing, she hugged her and said, "When I was your age, I was mischievous too! So, my darling daughter, let's do it together!"

They sorted the socks by colors, then by sizes, then into pairs, and they finished as the sun went down. Not a single sock was missing. Eight hundred and eighty-eight! But wait... except for one... Goldilocks' own pink sock, which a mother magpie had liked so much she took it to line her nest for her own pretty eggs to hatch on. She brought it back at the end of the summer, and Goldilocks found it on the raspberry patch, a little pink reminder of the day she first played with her new friend, Baby Bear.

Goldilocks and the Danger in the Forest

The Goldie family lived in a little house outside the town, and the bushy wood across their road was sunny and cool in summer and just right for building a snowman in winter. The Bears lived in a cottage further away up the road, where the wood was thicker with taller bushes and older trees. Goldilocks often went out of her garden and crossed the road to swing from some young oak trees, or chase the rabbits who came out of their tunnels to sit in the sun, but she sometimes wanted to explore deeper into the wood where the forest began. Baby Bear's wood was nearer the beginning of the forest, and deep inside the forest the trees grew thickly and so tall, said Papa Bear, that only the fierce Wild Bear, the Legend of the Forest, could climb to the top.

One fall morning, Wise Owl flew to Goldilocks' window on his way home to his oak tree. She woke up in surprise.

"You are late going home!" she told him. "I know," he replied, "I've been busy all night while you were sleeping. But something is happening in the forest. We are in danger!"

Goldilocks said, "I love danger! It's such fun!"

Wise Owl replied, "You are too mischievous, Goldilocks. Danger is not good at all!"

"Can I help?" asked Goldilocks.

"Yes, but please be wise, like me. I will tell you what I saw. Bad People are in the deep wood. They put a red ribbon on my oak tree! I do not like it at all."

Goldilocks suggested, "Maybe they are marking trees so that they don't get lost, like Hansel and Gretel in the story?"

"No," said Wise Owl. "They have handsaws and axes. I think they want to chop down my tree!"

13

"Oh no!" cried Goldilocks. "I will tell my Daddy – he's a doctor! He will stop them!"

"Thank you," said Wise Owl, "and now I will be off. I hope I have a good day's sleep!"

Goldilocks ran to her parents' room and shouted, "Wake up! Wake up! Danger!"

Her mother ran out. "Where?"

"In the deep wood! Bad people want to chop down Wise Owl's tree! Where is Daddy?"

"He is already working in the hospital," said her mother. "Jim Junior fell off a ladder and broke his leg last night!"

"We have to tell the Ranger!" shouted Goldilocks.

Her mom said, "Let's have breakfast, and then we will go into town to tell the Ranger."

Goldilocks was too impatient. While her mother was making scrambled eggs with chives, she ran out of the house and up to the Bears' house. Mama Bear was making pancakes.

"Baby Bear is still asleep," she told her.

Goldilocks bounded up the stairs and woke him up. "Quick, there's danger!" she told him. "We have to stop bad people from chopping down Wise Owl's tree!"

Baby Bear said, "First I want my pancakes."

Goldilocks ran out of the Bears' house and across the road into the wood.

"Wait," shouted Baby Bear, scrambling after her. "Wait for me!" He grabbed some pancakes, and when he caught up with Goldilocks, he stuffed them into her pocket.

Goldilocks slowed down when the bushes became thick and prickly. The two friends pushed their way through to a grassy knoll and found Dear Deer nibbling some low leaves.

"Where are you going?" she asked.

"There are bad people in the wood trying to chop down Wise Owl's tree and we are going to stop them!" said Baby Bear.

Dear Deer said, "That's deeper in the wood, where the forest begins. You might get lost."

Baby Bear said, "The forest! Oh no, I'm scared!"

Goldilocks said, "We will be fine! I know the way!"

Baby Bear agreed, "If you know the way, we will be fine."

The three friends set off between some old oak trees and reached the end of a narrow grassy path the Fox family had made by trotting along their favorite route. Mr. Fox was sitting under some fallen branches he had made into a door to his cave. "Where are you going?" he asked, peering out.

Dear Deer backed off. "Don't talk to him," whispered Baby Bear. "He's a wolf!"

"I am not a wolf," growled the fox. "Mangy, cowardly canines! Always in packs! We foxes are brave and hunt alone."

"Wise Owl's tree is in danger!" exclaimed Goldilocks. "Come and help us save it before the Bad People put red ribbons on your bushes too."

"With alacrity," said Mr. Fox, and shouted back into his den. "Leaving on a secret mission, Family! Do not stir from here, and eat your rabbit!"

Baby Bear shivered. "I told you not to talk to him!" he muttered.

Goldilocks replied, "He can't be bad, he has such a beautiful red tail!" She ran to keep up with him.

Baby Bear followed, nervously, with Dear Deer a little behind, lifting her head and sniffing the air as she picked her way, so carefully that she was nearly silent.

Some squirrels took an interest and began rushing from tree to tree. Rabbits hid in their underground tunnels, the fat old grouse put himself into a fuzz of old grass and only the prickly hedgehog followed along, grinning to himself.

"Mr. Sly Fox has joined us!" they whispered one to the other and soon some woodpeckers tapped out a warning: *Taptap tap tappety tap!* so that the mice would hear and keep away.

"Mr. Fox," said Goldilocks, "you are scaring all the other animals."

"You need me," laughed Mr. Fox, "to scare away the Bad People."

All the little animals nodded but they still kept a little away, and scuttled along underneath the deepest leaves.

Soon the trees around them grew taller and denser, until Baby Bear said, "Is this the forest?"

"Oh no," said Goldilocks, trying to cheer him up.

"Well, nearly," said Dear Deer, who liked to tell the truth.

"Yes, this is the forest," said Mr. Fox and all the mice squeaked, "Yes, yes this is the forest!"

Mr. Fox added, "But now you will see, I will scare away the Bad People! So do not worry!"

Soon they came to a little lake. Baby Bear was glad to see the sun shining on it and making the water glisten like silvery stars. An eagle was circling over the water, eyeing the fish he could see, and a family of twelve wild ducks were looking up and down in case the eagle decided to eat them instead of the fish. When they saw Mr. Fox, they splashed into the middle and quacked, "Danger! Danger!"

But Mr. Fox shouted, "Hey there Duckies! Have you seen any Bad People about?"

"Yes, YOU!" quacked one rude duck, but his sisters shushed him and shook their heads.

Eagle, who heard everything, called down, "Yes, Bad People are marking trees, keep walking and good luck, my friends!"

They all moved together through the forest. In the lead was Mr. Fox, then Goldilocks with Baby Bear just behind her, then came Dear Deer, a little to one side, listening and sniffing the air, and then all the other animals, some still under the leaves. Behind them waddled the ducks, because ducks are very inquisitive, a little like Goldilocks, but without very big brains.

After a while they heard a strange noise. Whack! Thwack! Klunk! Whoosh! Thud!

"Oh no," said Dear Deer, "I hear Bad People with axes. They are in the clearing, chopping down our trees!"

Down towards them swooped Wise Owl.

"They are heading back toward my tree," he said. "We need a plan."

"I have a plan," said Rude Duck. "Let's run away!"

"Shh, shh," said his sisters.

They all stood still while Goldilocks and Baby Bear whispered to each other.

"We will make a terrible noise, all together," she told him, "and then you rush over growling. They will be so scared they will leave!"

"But I'm only five!" groaned Baby Bear.

"Well, Fox will rush up showing his sharp teeth, Wise Owl will hoot into their ears, Dear Deer will jump at them, and the mice will run under their feet, so that they will be taken by surprise!"

"Good idea," said Mutti Duck. "Let's take them by surprise!"

"Yes," squeaked the mice, "we aren't afraid, we will also take them by surprise!"

Baby Bear said, "What will you do, Goldilocks? Are Bad People scared of little girls?"

"I don't know," she replied, solemnly. "But I will do my best. And Mr. Fox, please do not scare my friends or they will run away and we shall be all alone."

"I promise," grinned Mr. Fox. "Now, are we ready, Friends?"

"Ready!" they chorused.

"Ready, steady, GO!"

They all burst into the clearing, making the loudest noise any animals could make, and rushed up to five big Bad People with axes. Fox ran around biting their legs, mice ran under them so that they hopped and slipped, ducks flapped their wings and quacked, the grouse made them trip, Dear Deer jumped at them, Wise Owl and Eagle swooped up and down hooting and screeching, Hedgehog stuck out his prickles, and several buzzing insects joined in the battle, stinging and avoiding slaps. The Bad People fought back, but suddenly heard grunting. "It's a bear!" they shouted, and began to back off. Baby Bear grunted louder and louder, as his father had taught him forest bears do, but he kept hiding behind a bush, as he was only five. Then Goldilocks began singing in a high, strange voice, like a ghost in a story,

"Ahh," she sang. "Aah, aah *ooh*! The spirit of the forest is coming for *you*!"

The Bad People dropped their handsaws and axes and clung to each other. "No!" they cried. "Oh no!"

Then one of them said, "Wait, that's not a ghost, it's a little girl! And look, a baby bear and some mice!"

They picked up their axes again. The Friends became so scared they wanted to run, but the Bad People were no longer scared. Eagle and Wise Owl swerved over their heads, but they took no notice.

"Let's catch them!" shouted the Bad People.

"You can't catch us!" shouted Fox and Dear Deer.

The Bad People began to chase after the Friends, but then they stopped in their tracks. There was an enormous crash, a growl, a roar, and a huge, dark, hairy animal stood before them on two legs, with thick tufty arms and long sharp claws.

"Roooaar!" he threatened. "Rooooaaaar!"

The Bad People were terrified. The friends were terrified. Now what?

They all stood still, rooted to the spot. Goldilocks was the first to speak.

"Excuse me, but are you Wild Bear?"

"Yes," he growled at her. "I am Wild Bear, the Legend of the Forest."

Goldilocks, whose heart was beating fast, used her brains.

"Dear Wild Bear," she said. "we all wish to thank you so very much for winning this great battle. We are all grateful, aren't we, friends?"

Baby Bear and the other animals all squeaked, "Oh yes, we are so very grateful Mr. Wild Bear!"

Wild Bear nodded and said, "You all look good enough to eat. But I think I'll eat one of these Bad People first!"

Goldilocks gasped, "Oh Wild Bear, People don't taste good! Have you tried pancakes?"

Wild Bear frowned, "Now what are pancakes?"

"Here," she said, quickly emptying her pockets, "try this!"

Wild Bear took the pancakes and tasted them.

"Well, well, well," he growled. "This is the most delicious snack I ever had! Did you make this, Little Girl?"

Baby Bear stepped forward bravely.

"No, my Mama made them," he announced. Wild Bear looked at him, astonished.

"You have a Mama bear?" asked he asked. "I haven't seen a Mama Bear for a very long time! I want to meet your family, Baby Bear!"

Goldilocks and Baby Bear looked at each other. "If you promise to be good," they said, together.

Wild Bear stood over the Bad People and the mice tied so many twigs and bits of straw around them that they could only move their legs. They followed the friends through the forest and back into the wood, and there they found the Goldie Family, the Bear Family, Fireman Jim, the Ranger, and the Sheriff, all about to set off to find Goldilocks and Baby Bear.

When they saw the friends coming towards them, they began to cheer. The Ranger said to the Bad People, "Nobody is allowed to cut down trees in the Great Forest!"

The Sheriff said, "Now to teach you how to be good, you Bad People have to sweep up leaves and learn about the forest from the Ranger!"

The men said, "Oh no! We don't want to go to school!"

Everyone laughed, but suddenly they saw Wild Bear. They gasped, and shouted, "Oh no, Wild Bear, the Legend of the Forest!"

Wild Bear went up to Mama Bear and said, in his smallest voice, "Please Mrs. Bear, may I have some of your delicious pancakes?"

"Of course!" replied Mama Bear. "Come to our house, but only if you promise to be good!"

"I promise," he said, and they all trooped out of the wood, across the road and into the yard where they sat at a big picnic table and had a wonderful pancake party, everyone sharing, everyone friends.

Baby Bear and the Solar Eclipse

One morning, Baby Bear was in his garden, swinging from a branch, when he saw Wild Bear lumbering across the road towards him. "Wild Bear!" he shouted, "Come and play!"

Wild Bear stood by the gate and answered, "I don't feel like playing. I came to see you because I feel a bit scared."

"You? Scared?" answered Baby Bear, astonished.

"I know," said Wild Bear, seeming upset. "I looked around for Bad People, I looked for snakes and vultures and even wolves, but there was nothing scary anywhere!"

"Well, come and have some blackberries," said Baby Bear, "and you will feel better."

Wild Bear came into the house and Mama Bear gave him some berries in Papa Bear's big bowl.

After a bit, there was a snuffly noise, and Dear Deer stood at the door.

"I'm scared!" she sobbed. "I don't know why! There were no Bad People and no wolves, but I couldn't find Dad Stag, and all the rabbits are hiding!"

"Let's ask Papa Bear," Mama Bear advised. "He is making a winter ice house for his old mom and pop, but he'll be in soon. Let's sing, that will cheer you up."

They sang "Who's Afraid of the Big Bad Wolf," and "The Bear Came Over the Mountain," and after a while, Goldilocks arrived.

"Are you scared too?" asked Baby Bear.

"I'm never scared!" said Goldilocks. "But my mom and dad are going on a trip and I have to stay at home! It's not fair!"

"Where are they going?" asked Mama Bear.

"They are going to the North, with Teacher Tania and Fireman Jim and some other grown-ups. They left me with a babysitter and I'm not a baby! Not fair! They are going on a train! I've never been on a train!"

Mama Bear said, "You can stay with us. I am making hazelnut cookies. Everyone is singing. We will all help keep Dear Deer and Wild Bear from being scared."

"Oh, thank you!" said Dear Deer.

Wild Bear said, "But why are we scared?"

Just then Wise Owl flew by on the way back to his tree for his day's sleep.

"Something strange is going to happen," he told them. "I know, because the bats were all flying in the wrong direction all night!"

"Are you scared?" asked Dear Deer.

"No, not scared," replied Wise Owl. "But I think I'll stay here with you anyway… to keep you company!"

Suddenly Sly Fox rushed in, followed by Mrs. Gingie Fox. "May we stay with you for a while?" they asked. Their six Foxy children sat outside in a row, and Mama Bear's fat hen quickly hopped onto the window ledge and from there onto the roof.

"What a strange day!" said Mama Bear. "I will make enough hazelnut cookies for everyone!"

Goldilocks said, "I am not scared at all! But maybe the Grownups are scared, and that's why they are going North on a train!"

"No," said Mama Bear. "Your mom and dad are my friends. They would not leave you behind if anything scary was happening."

Goldilocks said, "So if it's not scary, why don't they let me come with them on the train?"

She was very cross and took a large handful of blackberries out of Papa Bear's big bowl. Baby Bear said, "Come outside and climb the tree. We can watch out for Bad People."

Mama Bear told him, "Baby, that's very brave of you! I am proud of you!"

Baby Bear and Goldilocks went outside, but Goldilocks said, "Baby Bear, I am going to run away and go on a train. Will you come?"

"I was on a train once," said Baby Bear, "when we came here from our home at the zoo. Maybe the grownups are going to visit my zoo!"

Goldilocks said, "Zoos are for kids who are five years old, like us. Let's go!"

She took Baby Bear's hand and they ran along the road and into her own house to get a jacket, because in the North it is cold. "Let's get some food," said Baby Bear. Goldilocks grabbed six cherry lollipops and added some chestnuts and apples, and by the gate she noticed a brown box with a label: "Special Glasses," so she shouted, "Babysitter, I'm taking this to my mommy!" And the two friends ran off just as Babysitter Gloria came running to the door, shouting "Stop! Come back! Come back!" But she was too late!

When they reached the train station, the platform was crowded with grownups and animals with their suitcases and they could not see Goldilocks' parents anywhere.

They searched up and down the platform but more and more people kept arriving. What a throng!

"All aboard for the Great Eclipse!" shouted the Stationmaster. He pushed Goldilocks and Baby Bear up the steps and into a compartment. They looked out of the window and waited for ages. Finally the Stationmaster blew his whistle. They sat down with some big furry dogs and a few goats wearing hats. Goldilocks held tight to the box of Special Glasses. The train choofed out of the station, left the town behind and began picking up speed through forests and mountains.

"Are you going to see The Great Eclipse?" woofed a Saint Bernard.

"We are going North!" answered Goldilocks.

"Then you will see the Great Eclipse!" chorused the goats.

"What's that?" asked Baby Bear.

"It's when the moon eats the sun until it goes black and the day becomes as dark as night!" answered a poodle.

"Oh no!" cried Goldilocks. "Now I understand why Mommy and Daddy left me at home!"

"Yes," said the biggest goat. "It is very scary. We don't usually let kids come on our adventures. But the sun always comes back. We all have to shout, *Come back Sun, come back Sun!* and then it does."

"My babysitter shouted, *Come back*," said Goldilocks, "and we didn't, so I'm scared the sun won't either. I want my mommy!" She began to cry.

"I'm scared too," said Baby Bear, "I'm only five!"

"Don't worry," said a mother goat with a beard. "If you can't find your mommy, I will look after you."

They all took out their snacks. Baby Bear, who was trying not to show that he was scared, ate half a chestnut, and Goldilocks sucked on a cherry lollipop.

The train chugged up and down mountains and finally reached the Station of the North. Everyone bundled out and stood on the platform. There were so many people! Goldilocks called "Mom! Dad!" but no one paid attention. Where were Daddy and Mommy Goldie?

Do you want to know what had happened at home?

I will tell you.

Back at the Goldie's house, Babysitter Gloria did not know what to do. She ran up to the Bears' house.

At that very moment, Papa Bear came in, saying "I have finished making the winter ice house for my old mom and pop, and I want Baby Bear to see it!"

Mama Bear called out, "Baby! Baby!" But just then Gloria rushed in crying, "Oh dear, help! Goldilocks and Baby Bear have run away!"

Mama Bear said, "Oh don't worry, they always go on adventures. They will be back soon!"

"No!" cried Gloria. "They took a big box of special glasses and ran to the station!"

Papa Bear said, "Oh no, they must be following Goldilocks' mom and dad – I heard that they are going on a train to see the Great Eclipse in The North!"

Gloria sobbed, "I am such a bad babysitter!"

Mama Bear said, "Now, Gloria, stop crying and help us find the children!"

They rushed out of the cottage and the animals raced after them, shouting, "Don't leave us alone!"

They ran past the Goldie's house, into the town and all the way to the train station.

The Stationmaster was blowing his whistle, and shouted "You are just in time! Climb on, we have to leave now!"

They all clambered onto the end of the train, just as it was starting to move.

"We did it!" they gasped and sat down to catch their breath.

The train chuffed out of the station and began to climb the mountains.

"I'm hungry," said Wild Bear.

"I'm hungry too," said all the Foxes.

Dear Deer began to cry. "Me too!" she said.

Mama Bear handed everyone hazelnut cookies, and out of the window they saw Wise Owl, flying as fast as he could alongside the train. "Whoo!" he called, "I hope we're nearly there!"

After a long while, the train reached the Station of the North and all the friends jumped out onto the platform. It was so crowded and noisy that they had to stand close together.

"Follow me, everyone!" shouted Papa Bear. "I'm going to look for Baby Bear and Goldilocks!"

Now I will tell you what was happening with Mr. and Mrs. Goldie, Teacher Tania, Fireman Jim, Mrs. Jim, and the Ranger.

They had no idea that Goldilocks or the Bears were on the same train. They stepped down and pushed their way through the crowd on the platform. Then they saw signs: "This Way!" and began walking up the steep path to meet the Space Scientist who was going to tell them about the Eclipse. At the top they saw the grand Observatory, with its big white dome and enormous telescope.

They were very excited. They stood together and Jim said, "Now let's check we have all our bags! Cameras?"

"Here!" called out Tania.

"Apple pie?"

"It's here!" replied Farmer Phil.

"Warm jackets?"

"I've got them!" called out Mrs. Jim.

"Eclipse glasses?"

Mrs. Goldie cried out, "Oh no!"

"What happened?" everyone asked.

Mrs. Goldie became very upset. "The glasses! I have lost the box of special Eclipse glasses!"

"Let's look on the train," said Daddy Goldie, and ran back down the hill, but the box was nowhere to be found.

He came back looking tired and very sad. "Now we won't be able to watch the Eclipse," he said.

Mrs. Goldie sat down on a rock.

"I am very, very sorry," she said to the other grownups. "I have spoiled everyone's trip. I'm just going to wait here until it's all over."

Suddenly she noticed Wise Owl flying past. "Wise Owl! What are you doing here?" she called.

"Look over there!" he hooted. Mrs. Goldie saw a head of curly golden hair coming towards her.

"Goldilocks!" she gasped and waved.

Goldilocks shouted, "Mommy! We came!"

Suddenly the Bears and all the animals pushed their way through the throng. "We came too!" they called.

"Hello everybody!" Goldilocks called. "Now we are all here to see The Great Eclipse! But why do you look so sad?"

"Oh dear," said her mother. "First, I can see you ran away from Babysitter Gloria, and second, I have lost the box of Special Glasses, so that means nobody can watch the Eclipse and our trip is ruined!"

Goldilocks laughed. Baby Bear began to laugh. His mama and papa laughed while Dear Deer, the Fox Family, and Wild Bear laughed so much that soon everyone at the Observatory was laughing happily.

"Mommy, I have the box of Special Glasses! Isn't it good that I decided to run away?"

Mrs. Goldie hugged her. Suddenly, the air became dark and cool, as if evening was arriving. Stars appeared. Little birds who had been hopping around chirping flew quickly back to their nests.

The bright sun looked like a white cookie with a black bite on one side.

All the animals began shivering again. "This Eclipse is scary!" they whispered, standing close together.

Mrs. Jim handed out jackets to keep everyone warm.

The Space Scientist called out, "Look, the Eclipse is starting! The moon is in the way so that the sun cannot shine on us!"

Then he shouted, "Everyone, put on your Special Glasses!"

All the people and animals put on their glasses and looked up at the sun. The dark bite grew bigger and bigger until the moon covered the whole sun, and everything went black.

"Now," called the scientist, "take off your glasses, but be careful – just for one minute!"

Everyone took them off and looked at the sun which had changed to a black ball, with flames coming out of it all around. Everyone gasped. "Oh, it's so beautiful!"

"Watch out for the tiny diamond!" said the scientist. "It's the sun trying to shine through the Mountains of the Moon!" Suddenly they saw a diamond sparkle at the side of the black sun, and the scientist said loudly, "Quickly, put on your glasses again!"

"Come back Sun, come back!" called the Goats.

Sure enough, the moon moved away and the sky was filled with sunshine. The little birds flew out again and Wise Owl hooted, "Silly day birds! I love night time!"

Everyone clapped their hands and cheered. The Great Eclipse was over, the Scientist had stopped the animals from being scared, and the two families and their friends sat on the grass by the Observatory. They opened the bags of cookies and snacks, and said to one another, "That was an amazing show! Let's come to the next Eclipse! And hurray to Goldilocks for bringing the box of Special Glasses!"

Baby Bear hugged Goldilocks.

"That was another exciting adventure," he told her. "You are my very best friend!'

"And you are mine," said Goldilocks.

Then they had a grand picnic, with apples, hazelnut cookies, chestnuts, while Baby Bear and Goldilocks ate all the cherry lollipops.

"Thank you!" everyone said, "You two saved the day! Hurray! Hurray!"

*   *   *

Baby Bear and Goldilocks are Babysitters

One very hot day, Mrs. Gingie Fox came into the Bears' house and said, "Please help me! I am so tired! My six pups at home are fighting and biting!"

"And smiting," sang Baby Bear, who loved to rhyme and sing.

"Baby Bear," said Mama, "do not be impolite to Mrs. Fox."

Mrs. Fox said, "Baby Bear makes funny rhymes, but my little cubs are really hard to handle. I tell them to play outside but they stay in our den and make too much noise!"

Mama Bear said, "Gingie, would you like Baby Bear to help you?"

Mrs. Fox replied, "What a good idea!"

Baby Bear said, "I am not a babysitter! I am only five!"

His mama said, "Go and play games with them. They think you are REALLY big, and they will listen to you!"

Baby Bear went to his room and found a box of games. He asked Mrs. Fox, "Will they like Snakes and Ladders?"

"Oh no," she replied. "They are afraid of snakes!"

"I will come after lunch," said Baby Bear. He was trying to think what he could do with the little foxes, and pretty soon he had an idea.

After lunch, he grabbed a bag of fresh plums his mama had picked that morning and ran along to Goldilocks' house. She was on her swing, trying to make a breeze to cool herself down.

"Goldilocks," shouted Baby Bear, "do you want to come with me to play with the little foxes?"

"No," replied Goldilocks. "It's too hot in their den. But we could play School under the cool trees in the Forest!"

"The Forest? Only if Wild Bear comes too," said Baby Bear.

Goldilocks noticed a tray of cupcakes her mother had just made for supper. She put them in a box, and the two friends, carrying the cupcakes and the plums, set off for the Foxes' den. On the way, they met Noble Stag, who was teaching Dear Deer how to eat bark off the trees.

"The Fox cubs?" he smiled. "I think you will need some help. My daughter will come with you."

"We are going into the Forest," said Goldilocks.

"Then do not get lost," said Noble Stag. "Deer Dear will help you find your way."

They walked into the Wood and saw Hedgehog. "No thank you," he said, when he heard where they were going.

They saw Wise Owl on his branch. "Go away," he grumbled. "It's daytime and I need to sleep!"

Some little mice followed them, giggling, as they thought it would be fun to watch the Foxes. Deer Dear kept saying, "Keep out of the way, you silly little things! I might tread on you!" But they just giggled even more.

In the Foxes' crowded den they found the six little cubs chasing around in the dark, biting each other's tails.

"Ooh, here is a scary human girl and a big fierce bear!" they yelled when Baby Bear walked in. He knew they were being silly. He decided they needed to learn how to respect other people.

"Come with us," he told them. "We are going on an adventure."

The little foxes ran outside and stopped when they saw Dear Deer. "Ooh, a giant Stag!" they jeered.

"This is Dear Deer," said Goldilocks. "She is very clever and will show us the way in the Forest."

The cubs followed the friends and snapped at the mice, who were too quick for them and hid in little holes only mice can see.

They marched through the wood that they knew so well, while the fox cubs pretended to be frightened, saying, "Ooh aah! So scary! We are so, so, so scared!" But soon they came to the dark trees and the Forest. They stopped talking. They pretended not to be frightened and kept closer together.

Soon they stopped at a mound of pine cones under a tall Redwood Tree.

"We are safe here," said Goldilocks.

"Now," said Baby Bear, "we are going to play School. I have made up a song. Everyone, stand and sing *Friends of the Forest Forever!*"

"We don't know that song!" the Foxes chorused.

Goldilocks stood up and sang the Anthem of the Forest:

The sun shines all day, the moon glows all night,
And nothing will change the dark or the light,
The clouds send us water and wintery snow,
The wind brings us weather, the ground makes things grow,
But humans and animals, birds, bugs and bees,
Depend on the forest of old wooden trees;
Their roots grow below and their branches above,
Their breath gives us air, yes, it's forests we love!

"Thank you!" said the tall Redwood tree. "I remember you saved us from the Bad People who wanted to chop us down. Listen to me!" She looked over the tops of the other trees and sang to the whole world:

Humans, animals unite,
Save us trees and do not fight!

The other redwoods and their cousins the pines joined in the chorus:

Our roots grow below and our branches above,
Our breath gives you air, yes, our Forests we love!

The little foxes sat in a row and looked up. The redwoods were so tall, they could not see the tops.

"Now," said Goldilocks, "before we eat plums and cakes, tell me what gives us fresh air to breathe?"

"Trees!" shouted the foxes.

Goldilocks laughed. "Yes, and why do trees have roots?"

"I know!" yelled Know-it-All Fox. "So we can dig holes under them! Now give us cupcakes!"

The tall Redwood shook itself so that seven pine cones fell off and bounced onto Know-it-All Fox's head.

"Ow!" he yelped. "I'm sorry! But my dad says your old roots make the best dens to live in, and he knows everything!"

A short pine tree nearby threw some pine needles at him.

"We Pine Family, Redwoods, and Firs," boomed the Redwood tree, "we *allow* you to dig dens between our roots!"

Three of the little foxes wanted the cupcakes, so they decided to be polite. They stood up and shouted, "Thank you!"

The other three began running round and round an old fir. "Silly old tree!" they giggled. "Stop!" groaned the fir. "You are making me dizzy!"

"Stop running!" shrieked the polite fox cubs. "Sit down or Redwood will bonk us again!" But the others just jumped on top of them and their fur began whirling around like leaves in the wind. Birds nearby flew away in fear. Dear Deer raced around shouting, "Stop!" The mice sat on a log cheering. Baby Bear tried grabbing their fluffy tails and Goldilocks jumped out of the way, as the foxes had sharp teeth. Wise Owl flew overhead, hooting angrily, "Who woke me up? What is all this hullabaloo?"

He sat on a branch and frowned. "Help is coming," he told Baby Bear.

Sure enough, there was a crash of branches, and Wild Bear appeared, glowering down at the battle.

Goldilocks dodged behind a White Pine and shouted, "Wild Bear! Help us, please!"

Wild Bear stepped into the midst of the fighting foxes. He picked up Know-It-All by his ear and Littlest Fox by her tail. The others stopped squabbling and huddled together.

Goldilocks stepped out and said, "We are visiting the Trees today, because they give us our homes. If we don't show them respect in their own home, they will not help us."

"Right," said a Spruce and threw some sharp pine needles down on them.

"Take these puppies away," creaked a White Pine.

"We are not puppies!" whined the Foxes. "We are fox cubs!"

"Then," boomed Wild Bear, "listen to your cubsitters, Goldilocks and Baby Bear!"

They sat down. Goldilocks whispered to Baby Bear, "Let's give them the cupcakes!"

"Yes," whispered Baby Bear, "and let's give Dear Deer the plums!"

"Fine," said Goldilocks. "My mom always says, *Feed the animals first!*"

Baby Bear whispered back, "My mama always sings a song called *Music Makes the World Go Round!* So first, let's sing!"

The two friends stood up and began singing the Anthem of the Forest again. The Fox cubs sang in high voices. Wild Bear and the trees joined in loudly, and Hedgehog, who had been listening secretly, began humming along. The birds flew back and warbled happily. Wise Owl hooted in the distance. The mice squeaked merrily. The breeze blew the branches and leaves fell gently on the happy animals. Then Dear Deer sang melodiously and nobody wanted to stop. When they had sung all the tunes they knew, Baby Bear and Goldilocks handed out the cupcakes, the mice scrambled for the crumbs, Dear Deer nibbled the plums, everyone called "Goodbye, Trees, thank you!" and trooped back to their homes.

When Baby Bear and Goldilocks arrived at the cottage, the two mothers and Gingie Fox were waiting at the gate.

"Goldilocks," called her mom. "Where are the cupcakes?"

"Oh no," said Goldilocks. "I gave them to the Fox cubs."

"Oh no," said Gingie. "Cupcakes are only for good cubs!"

"Oh no," said Mama Bear. "Where are the plums?"

"Oh no," said Baby Bear. "We gave them to Dear Deer!"

"So much food to keep children quiet! What terrible babysitters you are!" sighed the three mothers.

"Oh no, mama!" cried Baby Bear. "You always sing *Music Makes the World Go Round*, and that's what we taught them!"

"Yes!" chortled Goldilocks. "It was easy! Babysitting is my favorite job!"

"Oh no," replied her mother, winking. "Sorting socks is your favorite job!"

Goldilocks and Baby Bear began singing and everyone began laughing. They made up the words:

> *Let's all go sort out socks,*
> *Tra la la la la*
> *Let's all go sort out socks...*
> *Some socks are red and some are green,*
> *But we don't care as long as they are clean,*
> *We'll sing together and lose our cares,*
> *And the socks will fall into perfect pairs!*

"See?" said Goldilocks when they'd finished. "You were upset about the cupcakes, but look, we are all absolutely fine!"

"Ah," replied the mothers, smiling, "Cupcakes are really why the world goes round!"

Baby Bear and Goldilocks Go to School

Baby Bear was very excited. At the end of the summer he was going to start school.

His mama took him into town for a haircut.

"My," said the hairdresser, Helen of Troy, "you have a lot of fur!"

His mama said, "Do not cut off too much, please! He is a bear, not a boy!"

Helen of Troy trimmed the hair round Baby Bear's eyes and brushed his head. "Handsome!" she said.

She took the fur that she had cut off, put it into a blue box, and handed it to Mama.

"There," she said, "mommies like to keep their kids' first haircut!"

After the haircut, the bears stopped at the Goldies' house. Mommy Goldie was racing after Goldilocks with a brush. "Come here!" she called, but Goldilocks ran up to her room.

"Oh dear," she said. "Baby Bear, you look so neat, ready for school. I tried to braid Goldilocks' hair, but she would not sit still! Do you think Helen of Troy would try?"

Baby Bear went upstairs and found Goldilocks hiding under her colorful quilt. She peeped out and said, "I do not want braids, it hurts when my mom pulls them tight!"

Baby Bear said, "I just had a haircut."

Goldilocks asked, "Did it hurt?"

"No," replied Baby Bear. "Not a bit!"

Goldilocks got up and went to her arts and crafts drawer. She found a pair of scissors and said to Baby Bear: "Cut my hair!"

"I can't," he said. "My bear paws don't know how to use scissors!"

Goldilocks went to her mirror and snipped off a curl from over one ear. "That's a good idea," said Baby Bear.

The curl fell on the floor like a golden feather.

"Hmm," she said, "that's fine. Now I have to cut the other side." She snipped over the other ear and then some curls off the top of her head. Soon the floor was covered with golden locks.

Baby Bear picked up all the curls and put them in the waste basket.

They heard the two moms coming up the stairs. The two friends dived under the quilt to hide.

Mommy Goldie looked in the waste basket and screamed. "Oh no! Goldilocks has chopped off her head!"

Mama Bear rushed over to the quilt and found the two friends hiding. "Here she is!" she called.

"Why, oh why did you cut off your hair?" asked Mommy Goldie. "It was so golden and beautiful!"

Mama Bear said, "Baby, why did you let Goldilocks do it?"

Baby Bear replied, "She had scissors, so I thought it was a good idea!"

Mama Bear said, "I have a box for Baby Bear's hair to remember his baby fur. Can you put Goldilocks' hair in a box too?"

Mommy Goldie sighed, "Yes, I will. But now my little daughter looks too grown up!"

Goldilocks said, "Yes, now I'm ready to go to school!"

She went downstairs and there was her father coming home from his work. He saw his daughter's funny new hairstyle. Then he saw Mommy Goldie's sad face and knew he had to cheer her up.

"My," he exclaimed, "who is this little girl?" He was pretending he did not know her. He winked at Mommy and she felt better.

The next day Mama and Papa Bear walked Baby Bear all the way to the town school. On the way they met Goldilocks with her parents, and found lots of other children waiting by the school gate. Teacher Tania was standing by the gate, smiling.

"Welcome!" she called. "All five-year-olds, follow me!"

The children hugged their parents goodbye, and Teacher Tania led them to a big, sunny room. On the floor there were colored mats, and on the walls were pictures of trees and animals. Teacher Tania sat on the floor and called all the children to sit round her.

Baby Bear sat right next to her, because he remembered her from the trip to see the Eclipse.

"Hello, children!" she said. "Let's start by singing our names!"

She sang:

"Name, name, who's got a name?" and each person sang their name. There were names they knew, like Barry the Baker's son, Kid the Goat, Jim Junior's sister Janey, and Marcie Mayor. Goldilocks sang "Goldilocks!" Then it was Baby Bear's turn.

"Baby Bear!" he sang.

All the children laughed. "Baby! Baby!" they called. Baby Bear was upset. Goldilocks said, loudly, "He's my friend, so watch out or I won't be yours!"

The children stopped laughing. Teacher Tania said, "Goldilocks, I am very proud of you for being a good friend. Children! Friends do not hurt feelings. You know that already!" She said to Baby Bear, "Tell us about yourself!"

Baby Bear stood up and said,

"I was born in a zoo."

All the children said, "Cool!"

Baby Bear continued:

"When I was four, my keepers asked my Mama and Papa if we wanted to go out into the Big Wide World to teach people to respect other creatures and trees. We came here on a train and found our cottage near the forest. My Papa is learning to be a Ranger. He is very clever and made an ice house for my Grandmom and Pop, who are coming to stay with us during the winter. My mom writes stories about animals and she grows lots of berries."

Tania and the children clapped their hands.

Goldilocks stood up and said, "I was born here, I cut my own hair, my mom is great, my dad is great, and when I grow up, I'm going to be great." Then she sat down.

Tania said "That's great!" and all the children clapped.

There were more stories, then snacks, then playtime, then singing, and soon it was time to go home.

The parents were waiting for their children by the gate. They were all excited, but Baby Bear's mama and papa asked him, "Why do you look so sad?"

"I'm not sad," said Baby Bear. "But when I told them my name, they laughed! They kept calling me 'Baby.' I'm not a baby! I am five! Only Goldilocks stopped them. I am afraid they will laugh at me again."

Papa Bear said, "They do not know you yet. When they do, they will know you are not a baby. In the zoo, my name was Bobby, but when I came here, I told everyone it was Bob. So why don't we change your name just a little bit?"

Mama Bear sighed. "Oh, I love my Baby!"

Baby Bear said, "Please call me Little Bear!"

His parents said, "Good idea, but remember we loved you when you were a baby and always will, however big you grow!"

The next day at school, Baby Bear told everyone he had changed his name to Little Bear.

Kid the Goat said, "I saw Little Bear in the sky with my dad's telescope!"

"Yes," said Teacher Tania. She showed them a big picture of the stars.

"Look!" she said, "there are The Twins! And this is The Milky Way! But wait! Here are the ones called Little Bear!"

All the children said, "Cool!"

Every day was fun at school. Teacher Tania read stories and poems. The human children liked to hear about girls and boys like Cinderella, Jack and the Beanstalk and Alice in Wonderland, and the animal children liked The Three Little Pigs, Little Red Hen (they laughed so much), and The Ant and the Grasshopper.

Kid the Goat asked, "Why are there so many stories about bad wolves?"

Tania replied, "Wolves are not bad, but they like to stay together and that makes them feel important, so when they decide to go hunting they can be very fierce."

"Well, my mommy says never to talk to wolves," said Kid.

"My mom says that too!" squealed Piggles at the back of the class.

"There are bad animals, and there are bad people," said Tania. "We must find our good friends and look after each other."

Goldilocks said, "Yes, there are Bad People who tried to chop down our friends the trees!"

Teacher Tania said, "Tomorrow, Goldilocks, you and Little Bear can tell us how you saved the Forest."

The next day, the two friends told the class about their adventure in the Forest and how they met Wild Bear. Everyone listened, and said, "Cool!"

Then Tania said, "Now we are going to learn how to read!"

Everyone looked worried except Marcie Mayor, who began to sing "ABCD!" Soon they were all singing.

Tania said, "We will learn this way." She held up a picture of a tree and wrote the letters "TREE."

The children began to laugh. Tania turned around and there was an apple tree looking through the window!

After a while Tania hid the picture and just showed the word TREE. All the children shouted, "Tree!"

Soon she showed a picture of another tree. It was a pine tree. The children soon knew what the word TREE looked like, and the apple tree rustled its leaves saying, "Splendid!"

Tania showed pictures of oak trees, giant redwoods and mulberry trees.

Then she showed pictures of eagles and crows and owls with a sign "BIRD." She took away the pictures, and just showed the word.

"Bird!" everyone shouted. A robin on the apple tree tapped on the window and chirped, "Splendid!"

Later, everyone went outside to play in the yard. Goldilocks, Little Bear, and Piggles sat under the apple tree and called out, "Thank you, Tree!"

Piggles said, "I know some other trees like you, Tree. They live at Farmer Phil's apple farm."

"I know," said the tree. "My mom lives there. She gave an apple full of seeds to Dopey Horse and he dropped it here by the school. I was one of the seeds, and I grew up in the school yard learning to read! I am unique!"

"What does 'unique' mean?" asked Piggles

"It means I'm the only tree in the world who can read!"

Piggles shouted, "Tree, you are unique!"

"Well, I'm cool!" shouted Little Bear.

"And I'm just fine!" shouted Goldilocks.

Then Teacher Tania called: "Come inside, everyone!"

Goldilocks, Janey, and the other human children began reading lots of words without looking at any pictures. They were very excited.

Little Bear, Kid the Goat, Piggles and the other animals looked sad.

"We can't read yet, there are so many letters to learn!" they told Tania.

Tania smiled. She held up pictures of the trees, but this time without any words written on them.

"Now, animal children," said Tania, "do you know what these trees without names on them are called?"

Little Bear and the other animals all called out the names of every tree! "Oak!" they called. "It's so easy! Redwood! Cherry!" This time it was the human children who couldn't sort out which trees were which!

"We can't see any difference!" they said.

Goldilocks and Janey were surprised. "You are so good at knowing all the different trees!" they said to the Piggles and Kid.

Tania told them, "Every person in this school will be able to read. Some of you will read words quickly, some of you will learn to know which trees are which quickly. That is like reading, too! Perhaps you will know different plants. I am good at knowing the stars. And how wonderful if you will be able to hear all sorts of sounds no one else knows about. We will all learn something important: some things slowly, some things quickly, but the main thing is, we will all help each other."

Goldilocks said, "We will all be fine!"

Teacher Tania said, "That's good, Goldilocks, I'm happy you say 'fine'!"

When it was time to leave, Tania hugged everyone at the door, except for Piggles, who had got himself all muddy in the yard when they went out to play. "I am sorry, dear Piggles," she said, "but I have to keep my dress clean!"

Piggles looked sad. Then he thought of what Goldilocks would say if she were muddy.

"That's FINE!" he smiled. "My mom loves mud – she will hug me! We are the Perky Pig Family, you know!"

"I am proud of you!" Teacher Tania said, and everyone went home laughing and happy all the way.

*　　*　　*

Goldilocks and Little Bear's Amazing Vacation

On the last day of school, Teacher Tania told the children she could take five of them to Big City. They wrote their names on a piece of paper and dropped them into a box. Tania closed her eyes and picked out five names. Little Bear and Goldilocks were not chosen. They were very sad. But when Little Bear got home, his parents said, "Don't worry, we will have a wonderful vacation – we are going with Grandmom and Pop to see the Great Glacier in the North!"

"What's a glacier?" asked Little Bear.

"It's a river of ice," said Papa. "Grandpop's own parents were born there. They told me they grew up in a snowcave and loved rolling down the snowy hills!"

"Ooh, can Goldilocks come?" asked Little Bear, becoming excited.

"If her mom and dad say she can!" agreed Mama and Papa.

Little Bear rushed to Goldilocks' house. She was jumping up and down shouting, "Hurray! We are going South to Flowerland to see the alligators! Can you come with us, Little Bear?"

Of course, both friends had to stay with their parents. They were sad not to be together. "It won't be fun without you," they told each other. When the day came to leave, Little Bear said, "When we come home, let's meet at Farmer Phil's Apple Farm. You love apples, and I love apple pie!"

At the station, Teacher Tania and five children were climbing into the train going to the Big City. Little Bear felt very lonely watching his school friends leave, but Grandpop lifted him up to wave goodbye. After a few minutes, along came the Train to the North. The Bear Family sat down

and the train chugged away from the town, through meadows and forests, alongside roaring rivers and up snowy mountains until it reached The North. Finally, the family climbed out and sat in a sleigh pulled by barking fluffy-furred Husky dogs who took them across the snow all the way to Glacier Hotel.

Little Bear began to enjoy the vacation. He chatted to the Huskies who told him to be very careful on the glacier. "Don't walk around by yourself!" they barked.

Meanwhile, Goldilocks and her parents had climbed onto the train to Flowerland. The further south they went, the weather became hotter and hotter, but at every station her father bought her ice-cream. "I like this vacation!" she cheered and her mother said to her dad, "Oh no, honey, ice-cream is only for special treats!" but she laughed too, as she was going to see The Famous Flower Show.

Finally they arrived. At the station they took a taxi to the Gator Hotel, overlooking a green and watery swamp. "Be careful by the swamp!" said the driver. "Don't go walking by yourself!"

Meanwhile, Goldilocks and her parents had climbed onto the train to

The next day, in the North, Little Bear woke up very early. He was too excited to eat breakfast. He rushed out of the hotel and rolled about in the snow. Then he stepped down onto the glacier. It was like standing on an ice rink. In the distance he saw a big white Polar bear who was waving his paw at him. The ice looked so smooth! "I want to skate to the other side," he thought, "and talk to Mr. Polar. I can be back before breakfast!"

He looked down at his feet, and to his surprise he saw the ice he had been standing on had moved a little away from the land. "So that's why Mr. Polar was waving," he thought, and wanted to jump back onto the snow. But the ice floor had moved even more. Suddenly there was a sharp cracking sound and the floor became an ice-island surrounded by water! It split again and began moving faster down the river.

Mr. Polar shouted, "Swim, Little Visitor!"

"I can't swim," cried Little Bear.

"You must try!" shouted Mr. Polar, jumping towards him, but the ice he was on split too, and he had to swim back to the snow.

The ice-island moved faster and faster with Little Bear stranded on it, so that first he saw the Glacier Hotel disappear, next the snowfield he had been rolling in, and then he found himself surrounded by water. "Help!" he shouted, waving, but only gurgling ravens saw him.

Nearly all the ice melted and Little Bear was on his ice-island, whooshing down the river, sloshing round rocks and whirling in whirlpools. A raven flew overhead croaking, "Waterfall ahead! Jump off, Little Brown Bear! Swim!"

Little Bear looked down and saw that on one side of the ice-island the water was fast and but on the other it had slowed down between a group of rocks with low branches hanging over their sides. He reached out, grabbed a branch and swung up onto a rock, while the ice-island whirled away and hurtled towards the waterfall where it fell into a thousand glistening pieces.

"Whew! I'm safe!" he thought, and jumped from rock to rock until he reached the land and the tall Northern pine trees. "Now which way to go?" he wondered.

"That-a-way to the South!" rustled the leaves.

"That-a-way to the sun!" bellowed a mighty elk, who was very surprised to see him.

"Hedgehog Land is that-a-way!" grunted a porcupine. Little Bear wanted to talk to these animals but they all seemed to want to help him find his way home.

"Thank you!" he shouted.

He walked so long all day that he fell asleep under a bush. When he woke, it was morning and a familiar voice was calling. It was Eagle from the forest at home!

"The robins called out the news and all the different Bird Bands sang about it from treetop to treetop until I heard it in my nest," said Eagle. "Noble Stag is on the way to bring you back to our land. I'll tell the sparrows to tell the robins to tell the ravens to tell your parents that you've made it safely home."

After an hour, there was a great commotion, and through the bushes came Noble Stag, followed by Wild Bear, panting from the run. "I am so happy we found you!" he growled, hugging his little friend.

"Hop onto my back," said Noble Stag, "and home we go."

After many hours, with some stops to eat blackberries, they arrived at the Bears' house. Wild Bear climbed an oak tree to nap, and Noble Stag ran back into the forest. Little Bear went into the kitchen, but the mice had squeezed in to steal the food and there wasn't a crumb left. "I am so hungry!" he said to himself. "I want pancakes or sandwiches or mushroom soup! I wonder if Goldilocks's family is home yet?"

He ran to the Goldie's house, but they too were still on vacation and all the doors were locked. He ran into town, but everyone was away, and even Fireman Jim was taking a day off. Suddenly he remembered his promise to Goldilocks to meet at Farmer Phil's Apple Farm. "Hmm, apple pie!" he thought. He set off up the lane and soon came to the farmhouse.

* * *

Now let's leave Little Bear and go to the South to join Goldilocks in Flowerland.

Goldilocks also got up very early, before anyone else was awake. She ran out of the Gator Hotel down to the water. It was a hot day. The sky was blue and a strange white bird with long skinny legs was striding about in the weeds. "Hello Visitor," he said. "What would you like for breakfast? A shrimp? A baby alligator?"

"Oh, no thanks!" Goldilocks laughed. "Can you fly?"

"Of course I can fly, I'm a whooping crane," said the bird. "Whoop! Whoop!" And he took off over the water.

"Wait!" shouted Goldilocks. "I am sorry I was rude to you!"

At that moment she saw other birds lifting off from the ground and trees and flying away from the water.

"Don't be frightened of me!" shouted Goldilocks.

"We aren't frightened of you!" screeched the birds, flapping away into the distance. "Go into your People house, little Visitor! The big wind is coming!"

Goldilocks looked up but saw only blue skies. A pelican walking by with a fish hanging out of his mouth swallowed the poor thing and called, "The Big Wind! Run indoors, little Person!" He then lifted himself off and flew away from the water.

Suddenly a grey cloud filled the sky and a wind began to blow.

"I must first see the alligators," thought Goldilocks. She ran down close to the water and saw some alligator eyes and noses sticking up into the air. One big alligator lifted his head and called out, "Hide, little Human!" and sank under the water weeds.

The sky grew darker and the wind stronger. Goldilocks' curls blew into her eyes so that she couldn't see her way. She began running back towards the Gator Hotel, but suddenly a really strong wind gust hurled her backwards. She struggled towards a sturdy oak but couldn't hold on to its thick trunk, so she staggered towards a slim trunk. "Girl, don't hold that Palm trunk!" called a huge ironwood, "hold me!"

"I can't, you are too far away!" Goldilocks shouted with the wind whishing into her ears, and wrapped her arms round the slender palm trunk, holding on tightly while the wind hurled itself round the garden and whirled leaves and branches in circles.

"Oh no!" squeaked the palm, and Goldilocks felt it lift into the air and take off over the roof of the hotel!

She shut her eyes and thought, "This is just a dream, I'm still in bed!" But when she opened her eyes, she was high in the air grasping onto the trunk with all her might.

"Hold tight!" shouted the palm, "I hope we don't land anywhere dangerous! But this is amazing, I'm a flying palm tree!"

Goldilocks shouted back, "And I'm a flying girl!"

They were pushed hard by the great wind, high over cities and hills, up, up and round and round while below them they saw other flying objects like bushes and trashcans, flags and even garden gnomes, who didn't care at all because they weren't alive.

"We are having fun!" screamed the palm.

The wind blew them north and over a rushing river, but after many hours it began to slow down over a forest. Goldilocks shouted, "I know where we are! This is my forest!"

The wind stopped and the tree landed near where the wood began, between two white pines.

"Oh goodness, what in the world are YOU?" asked one pine impolitely to the palm. "Goldilocks, you are so mischievous! You make friends with such strange creatures!"

The palm stood up proudly.

"I am a Queen Palm," she announced. "I come from Flowerland, and I brought my little friend home safely!"

"Oh, Your Majesty," said the other pine. "Thank you for saving Goldilocks! She saves trees and now you have saved her!"

Other trees nearby leaned over to look at Queen Palm. "We have never seen such a strange tree!" they whispered.

Wise Owl flew up and hooted, "Thank goodness you are safe, Goldilocks! Eagle heard about the Wind and knew you would get up to mischief! But Your Majesty Palm, it is not safe for you here. Our weather is warm now, but we have icy winters."

"What is ice?" asked Queen Palm.

No one could explain ice and snow to her. She began to giggle.

"It sounds like ice cream," she told them. "I see children eating it all the time. It must be delicious!"

The trees groaned. "Queen Palm must go home," they told each other.

Goldilocks said, "I will go find Fireman Jim. He has a big truck and can drive her back to Flowerland."

She set off, helped by the trees who nodded their heads to show her the way. When she reached the road, she began to feel hungry. She ran past the Bears' house to her own house but the mice had crept into her kitchen too, and eaten every cake and even the flour and raisins to make the cake, while on the floor lay broken egg shells left by sneaky squirrels who had come down the chimney.

"Why does everyone call me mischievous?" she said to herself. "Squirrels and mice are much naughtier than I am!"

She ran up the road and into the town, but she, like Little Bear, found no one at home, not even Fireman Jim. Only his old horse, Dopey, was standing behind the firehouse, eating hay.

"Do you have any apples?" he asked her.

"Apples!" she exclaimed. Suddenly she thought of Farmer Phil and how she had promised to meet Little Bear at the apple farm when they got home.

She jumped on Dopey Horse and said, "Please, Dopey, take me to Farmer Phil's farm! There are lots of apples there!"

Dopey trotted the way she showed him, and she arrived at the farm to see none other than her best friend, Little Bear, sitting on the gate and eating a Red Delicious. "You came!" shouted Little Bear. "You remembered!" shouted Goldilocks.

They went into the farmhouse and Mrs. Phil gave them each a huge slice of apple pie. "Do your parents know you are home?" she asked.

"Oh dear, no," replied Goldilocks.

At that moment, Eagle looked in through the window.

"I told the news that you are safe to my friends the crows, and they said they told the mockingbirds, who told the cranes near Flowerland, so by now your parents will know you are here."

"Oh, thank you!" cried the friends.

Mrs. Phil tucked them under a soft quilt in her spare bedroom and when they woke up, in rushed the Goldies and the Bears, with hugs for their children. "We were so worried!" they said. "We were going to bring back some plants to put in Mommy Goldie's new hothouse – you know how she loves gardening, even in the winter! But we came home so suddenly we couldn't bring anything."

"Wait," cried Goldilocks, "can we plant a Queen Palm tree?"

"If I can fit her in my hothouse!" smiled her dad.

They all walked to the forest, where they found Queen Palm chatting about colorful parrots and toothy alligators to the other trees, who did not believe a word she said. Fireman Jim and Wild Bear arrived to meet her. Then everyone pulled and heaved her all the way to the Goldie's house, where Daddy Goldie showed her the beautiful tall hothouse. Queen Palm stood in it saying, "Now I will be able to see the ice cream covering the land in the winter!"

"Really?" said Dopey Horse, who believed everything. Everyone began laughing.

"Well," said Mama Bear, "the weather was terrible, you were both very mischievous, and we had to come home early, but we are so happy to be safe and all together. You will never forget your amazing vacation!"

"Yes," smiled Goldilocks, "everything always turns out just fine!"

"Tomorrow we'll go shopping for flour and make more apple pie," said Mommy Goldie.

"Good idea!" squeaked the mice.

Goldilocks and Little Bear went upstairs to play. The Goldies and the Bears sat at the table drinking blackberry cordial.

"Ah," said Mr. Goldie, smiling. "I'm so happy the children are safe!"

"Yes," replied Mr. Bear, "it's so nice and quiet now!"

After a few minutes, Mrs. Bear said, "Hmm, it's a bit too quiet!"

Mrs. Goldie ran up the stairs and opened the door.

On the floor she saw Goldilocks' colorful quilt and under it was Wild Bear, fast asleep.

He woke up and yawned.

"They climbed out of the window for a little adventure," he told her. "But don't worry, you can always ask me to save them if they get into mischief! Little Bear and Goldilocks together will always, always, be absolutely fine!"

* * *

CPSIA information can be obtained
at www.ICGtesting.com
Printed in the USA
LVHW072127230222
711865LV00004B/20

9781636613376